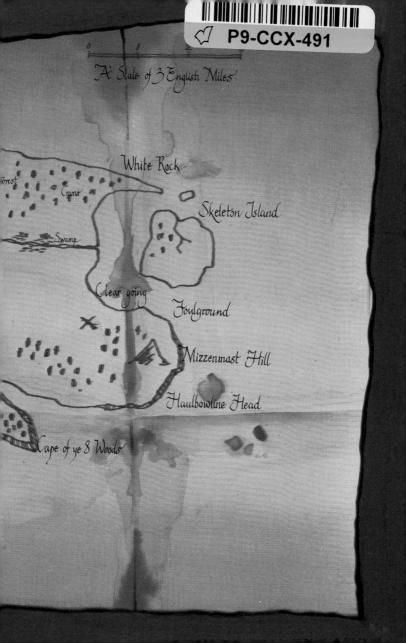

With a changing world, adventure stories change too, but Treasure Island *is one which will always be read wherever there are children to be fascinated by the idea of buried treasure and the tussle between good and evil. It is one of the greatest adventure stories ever written.*

TREASURE ISLAND

Robert Louis Stevenson

retold in simple language
by Joyce Faraday
with illustrations by Dennis Manton

Ladybird Books Loughborough

Treasure Island

I remember, as if it were yesterday, the old seaman who came to live at our inn. He was tall and strong and his black pigtail hung on his shoulders. His hands were rough and he had a white scar across one cheek. His name was Billy Bones and when he was drunk, as he often was, we were all afraid of him. He never talked to any of the sailors who called at the inn, and he paid me fourpence a month to warn him if I should ever see a sailor with one leg.

My father was ill at the time and I was left to look after Billy Bones. He drank so much that Dr Livesey warned him that rum would kill him. But he didn't care to change his ways and, when he lay weak and helpless in his bed, he told me a bit about himself.

He had been the mate on board the pirate ship of Captain Flint. When the captain was dying he had given Billy Bones the map that showed where his treasure was buried. Since that day the rest of Flint's old crew had tried to get hold of the map. It was hidden in Billy Bones' sea-chest.

One frosty afternoon an old blind seaman, Blind Pew, called at the inn. He gripped Billy Bones' hand as he left and something passed from his hand to Billy's. I saw the fear in Billy's eyes when he looked into his hand.

'The black spot!' he cried. 'Jim Hawkins, listen to me. This black spot means that my old shipmates are coming to get me. They're after my map, Jim! They'll kill me!' He sprang up as he spoke and the strain and shock must have been too much. He fell dead at my feet.

Billy Bones died without paying his bills. My mother and I took from his sea-chest some of his money to pay what he owed. There was also a bundle of papers which I took for safe keeping.

That very night a gang of ruffians attacked our inn. My mother and I hid outside and watched as they searched Billy Bones' sea-chest. Unable to find what they wanted, they shouted and raged. I realised that the bundle of papers in my pocket was what they were after.

I went to Dr Livesey and Squire Trelawney
and told them the whole story. When we
opened the bundle we found Captain Flint's
treasure map, and the Squire was very

excited. 'Flint was the most bloodthirsty pirate that ever sailed,' he cried. 'I'll fit out a ship in Bristol! I'll take you, doctor, and you too, Jim Hawkins, and some of my men. We'll have that treasure!' So it was that Squire Trelawney bought the *Hispaniola* and prepared her for the voyage. He needed a good crew, and took on a one-legged sailor named Long John Silver as ship's cook. This man was very helpful to the Squire and picked out some tough men to work the ship. In a few weeks the *Hispaniola* was ready to sail away.

We set sail under our captain, Captain Smollett. I was ship's boy. The coxswain, Israel Hands, was an able man, and Long John Silver was a fine cook. He carried his crutch on a cord round his neck so that both his hands were free. He propped himself against the side and got on with his cooking like someone safe ashore. We all worked well and willingly, and I often heard the crew singing as they worked. The song was one I'd heard from old Billy Bones.

'Fifteen men on the Dead Man's Chest – Yo-ho-ho and a bottle of rum!'

I passed many spare moments in Silver's shining galley where his parrot, Captain Flint, swung in its cage. It was named after the pirate and all day long it screeched, 'Pieces of eight! Pieces of eight! Pieces of eight!' Silver was interesting company, full of gripping yarns of other voyages and adventures. He was well-liked by all and the men looked on him as a leader.

On deck we kept a barrel of apples for the men to help themselves. One evening I went to the barrel and, finding it nearly empty, climbed inside to get an apple from the bottom. There I sat, quietly rocked by the sea. Someone sat down on the deck and leaned against the barrel and started to speak. The words I overheard made my blood run cold. Israel Hands and Silver were planning to take over the ship once we had found the treasure. They would kill the captain and any of us who would not fall in with them! I could not believe my ears.

There was a sudden shout of 'Land-ho!'
The men all ran to catch a first sight of land.
I took the chance to jump out of the barrel
and join the rest. Captain Smollett was
telling the crew about the island. Long John
Silver said that he'd been there before when
his ship had put in for water. I looked at his
smiling face and shuddered. I now knew
that Silver was more than a cheerful ship's
cook. He was also a bloodthirsty pirate! As
soon as I could slip away I told the captain
and my friends, the Squire and the doctor,
what I had heard. They decided we were
safe until the treasure was found. There were
nineteen pirates, but only seven of us. When
we were ready we would surprise them, and
hope to win by catching them unprepared.

We now lay off Treasure Island. It looked
a gloomy, forbidding place. The lower parts
were wooded, with rocky peaks jutting
above the trees. Even in the sunshine, with
birds soaring above, I hated the thought of
it. We were anchored in an inlet where trees
came down to the water. The air was hot
and still, and the men were restless and
grumbling. Captain Smollett gave leave for
the men to go ashore, which raised their

spirits. I believe the silly fellows thought they would break their shins over treasure as soon as they landed. Long John Silver was in charge of the two boats taking thirteen men ashore. I knew I should not be needed on board and decided to go ashore too.

I ran up the beach into the woods, glad to be free and alone. I sat quietly hidden in the bushes. Hearing voices, I moved nearer to catch the words. I could see and hear Silver bullying a sailor to join the pirates. The sailor angrily refused. Silver's answer was to plunge his dagger into the man and leave him lying dead in the forest. I felt faint, and the whole world swam from me in a whirling mist. When I pulled myself together, Silver, crutch under his arm, was wiping his knife on a tuft of grass. I feared for my life if I should be found, and ran and ran, not caring where.

When I stopped I was at the foot of a stony hill. My eye was caught by a movement on the hillside. I could not tell if it was a man or an animal. Here was a new danger I felt I could not face, and I began to run towards the shore. But the creature was faster than me and, darting from tree to tree, he came closer. I could see now that it was a man, but so wild and strange that I was afraid. As he neared me he threw himself on the ground, and held up his hands as if begging for mercy.

My courage returned and I spoke to him.
'Who are you?' I asked.

'I'm poor Ben Gunn, I am,' he answered.
'It's three years since I spoke to anyone.' I
had never seen such a ragged creature. He
was dressed in a patchwork of odd clothes
and goatskins, and his blue eyes looked
startling in a face burned black by the sun.

He told me he was rich, and babbled away
in a high, squeaking voice. Sometimes he
spoke sense and sometimes his words had
no meaning. I felt he might be a little crazy
after being alone so long. He said that he'd

been on Captain Flint's pirate ship and that three years before he had come back with some seamen to look for Flint's treasure. When they could not find it the sailors went off, leaving him alone on the island. When he'd seen our ship he'd thought that Flint had returned.

I told him Flint was dead, but that some of Flint's old shipmates were among our crew. When I spoke of Silver, his face filled with terror. I told him we should have to fight the pirates, and he promised to help us if we would take him back home with us.

Our talk was interrupted by gunfire, and
we ran towards the sound. Among the trees
we came upon a high wooden fence which
ran round a cleared space in the forest. I
could see the Union Jack flying from a
strong log-house in the clearing. I knew that
my friends must have left the ship and were
defending themselves in the log-house. The
battle with the pirates had begun! The
Hispaniola lay in the inlet with the Jolly
Roger at her mast. On the beach a group of
drunken sailors lolled on the sand.

I parted from Ben Gunn and climbed the stockade to join my friends in the log-house. They were delighted to see me, for they had feared for my safety. Dr Livesey told me what had happened after I had left the ship. The captain had decided that the time had come to fight it out with the pirates. From Flint's treasure chart he knew about the log-house. Dr Livesey and one of our men had rowed ashore to find it. There was a fresh water spring by the house and the high fence made it a good place to defend. They then returned to the *Hispaniola* to collect the rest of the faithful crew. They had loaded a small boat with food and ammunition and made a dash for the shore.

There was a small group of pirates
still on board the ship. When they saw
what was happening they had opened fire
on the little boat and it had sunk in shallow
water. The Squire's party had waded
ashore but lost half the stores and

gunpowder. The doctor was sure the pirates would soon give up the fight. He said they would get ill from too much rum and with disease from their swampy camp-site.

I told my friends what had happened to me, and of my meeting with Ben Gunn. Dr Livesey wanted to know all about him, for we clearly needed help. The three leaders of our party were at their wits' end what to do. We had little food and the pirates could soon starve us out. I was worn out at the end of a hard day and soon fell asleep.

In the morning I awakened to the sound of bustling and voices. Long John Silver himself was approaching the stockade carrying a white flag. Captain Smollett suspected a trick and ordered us to be ready to fire. Silver said he had come to make terms to end the fighting. He was allowed to come inside the stockade. He threw his crutch over, got a leg up and cleverly dropped inside the clearing. He came and sat down outside the log-house, and told the captain that the pirates intended to get the treasure. He said that, in exchange for the treasure map, he would take us off the island to some safe place.

Captain Smollett was not the man to make terms with pirates. Angrily, he told Silver that he and the pirates were done for. Without the map they had no hope of finding the treasure. With or without the treasure, not one of them could plot a course to sail the ship home. He ordered Silver out of his sight. Fury blazed in Silver's eyes, and, with curses and threats, he disappeared into the wood.

We now prepared for the coming attack, and sat and waited in the baking heat. Suddenly, musket shots hit the log-house,

and pirates leapt from the woods and climbed the stockade. Shouts and groans, shots and flashes filled the air. I grabbed a cutlass and dashed outside to join in the fight. In moments we had fought them back. Those who were not killed or injured scampered to the woods for shelter. We ran back to the log-house to take stock. We knew there must be a second attack. We had lost two men and the captain was badly injured. We waited and watched, but all remained quiet.

In the lull, I saw Dr Livesey slip quietly out of the stockade. I guessed he was going to find Ben Gunn. Still no attack came and I grew weary of waiting. The heat, the blood and the dust made me restless and I longed to get away to a cool, fresh place. I knew the captain would never let me leave the stockade. When no one was looking I put two pistols in my pocket and slipped out.

I ran to the shore and felt the cool wind and watched the surf tumbling and tossing its foam along the beach. Climbing a hill, I could look down on the calm inlet where the *Hispaniola* lay on a flat sea. In a little boat beside her I could make out Long John Silver. He was talking and laughing with two men on the ship. No words reached me, but the screeching of Silver's parrot was carried on the wind. About sundown, Silver shoved off for the shore and the two men left on board went below deck. I was sure that if the pirates could not find the treasure they would sail away without us. A plan began to grow in my mind.

Ben Gunn had told me that he had made a boat and hidden it near the shore. If I

could get to the *Hispaniola* I could cut her
anchor ropes. She would drift away to
another part of the shore and the pirates
would be unable to escape from the island.
I searched in the bushes and, to my joy,
found the hidden boat. It was made of
goatskin stretched over a wooden frame,
and it was so flimsy I wondered if it was
strong enough or big enough to hold me.
With darkness, fog crept into the inlet. It
was a perfect night for my plan. I pushed
away from the shore and drifted silently
towards the *Hispaniola*.

As I came alongside the ship I could hear loud, drunken voices. Israel Hands was shouting at another man. They were not only tipsy, it was plain they were also angry. On the shore I could see the glow of the fire in the pirates' camp. Someone there was singing the song I'd heard so often before —

'Fifteen men on the Dead Man's Chest —
Yo-ho-ho and a bottle of rum!
Drink and the devil had done for the rest —
Yo-ho-ho and a bottle of rum!'

Strand by strand, I cut the anchor rope and the ship began to swing and slide away to the open sea. As she slid past me I could see into the cabin. Israel Hands and the ship's watchman were fighting. They were too busy to feel the movement of the ship. I was in great danger and I lay flat in my little boat, praying I should not be seen.

For hours, it seemed, I was tossed on the waves and I must have slept, for it was broad daylight when I awakened. My boat had drifted along the coast but I could see no landing place under the rocky cliffs. I could only let my boat drift on and hope to find a sandy shore. The hot sun and the salt from the sea-spray had given me a raging thirst. I wanted to be on shore in the cool shade of the trees. As I rounded a headland the sight before me made me forget my cares. No more than half-a-mile away lay the *Hispaniola*! Her sails were set but, by the way she turned and drifted, it was clear no one was steering her. If the pirates were drunk and I could get aboard her, I might be able to capture the ship!

I paddled fast but with the wind filling her sails, the *Hispaniola* kept her lead. At last I had my chance. The breeze fell and she turned in the current and stopped. I came alongside and leapt aboard. The wind took her sails and she rushed down on a wave and sank my little boat. I had no way of escape now. I moved quietly on the deck among empty bottles. Not a soul was to be seen.

At length I saw two pirates. One was
clearly dead, lying on the blood-stained
deck. The other was Israel Hands, wounded
and groaning and unable to stand. When he
saw me he begged for brandy to ease his
pain. I went below into the wrecked cabin
to find some brandy and after a drink,
Hands seemed stronger.

I agreed to give him food and to patch up his wounds if he would tell me how to steer the ship into a safe harbour. For the time being, he needed me to help him and I needed his help to save the ship. But I did not trust his odd smile as he craftily watched me. He asked me to fetch some wine from the cabin and when he thought I had gone below, he staggered painfully across the deck and picked up a knife which he hid in his jacket. This was all I needed to know. Israel was now armed and I knew he meant to kill me as soon as we had brought the ship ashore.

The beaching was difficult. It took all my care for I did not want to damage the ship and so I was too busy to keep watch on Hands all the time. Suddenly, I was aware of danger. Perhaps I had heard a creak or seen a shadow moving with the tail of my eye, but, sure enough, when I looked round, there was Hands already half-way towards me. A dagger was in his right hand. I dashed away and pulled a pistol from my pocket. Turning, I took aim and fired. There was no flash, no sound. The powder was wet with sea-water. The ship gave a sudden lurch as she hit the shore and we were both thrown off our feet. Before Hands could stand again, I had climbed the mast. Safe for the moment, I sat in the rigging and put dry powder in my pistols. Hands was slowly coming up the mast. His dagger between his teeth, he dragged himself after me.

'One more step, Mr Hands,' I called, 'and I'll blow your brains out!' He stopped and in a flash flung his dagger. I felt a sharp pain and found myself pinned to the mast by the shoulder. The sudden pain and shock made me fire both my pistols. With a cry,

Israel Hands fell head first into the water. I felt sick and faint and shut my eyes until I became calm. When I had freed myself, I found that the wound was not very deep in spite of the blood that ran down my arm. In the cabin I found bandages to bind up my wound.

It was now sunset and I waded ashore.
All I wanted was to be back with my friends.
I hoped that the capture of the *Hispaniola*
would be enough for them to forgive me for
having left them. The moon helped me to
find my way to the stockade. I walked
carefully and silently and dropped over the
fence. There was no sound. The man on
watch had not heard me. I crept to the

log-house and stepped inside. Suddenly a shrill voice rang out in the darkness. Flint's parrot screeched, 'Pieces of eight! Pieces of eight! Pieces of eight!' Instead of finding my friends, I had come face to face with the pirates! By the light of a flaming torch I saw Silver and the five men who were still alive.

There was no sign of my friends, and my first thought was that they had all been killed. But I soon learned that this was not so.

While I had been away, Dr Livesey had gone to the pirates and told them that, because the ship had gone, he and his party had given up the search for treasure. The log-house and everything in it, even the treasure chart, was handed over to the pirates and my friends had walked out into the woods.

This news puzzled me. I could not understand why they had given up without a fight.

Long John Silver was still the pirate leader, but he seemed less cheerful than before. It was clear that the men did not obey him willingly. If they should pick a new leader, Silver knew they would kill him. His only hope of being saved was to be on Captain Smollett's side.

He promised to protect me from the pirates if I would put in a good word for him with the captain. But if the pirates guessed he had changed sides, I knew they would finish us both. Our lives depended on keeping our plan secret.

The next morning, Dr Livesey came to the log-house to see to the sick and wounded. He was surprised to see me with the pirates but he said nothing. He went on his rounds giving out medicine and dressing wounds. When he had finished, he asked to speak to me alone. As fast as I could, I told the doctor of all that had happened to me. When he heard that the *Hispaniola* was safe his eyes opened wide in amazement. I told him of Silver's danger and he agreed to take him home with us if he would keep me safe. We were in a tight corner and it looked as though there was little hope of getting out of it. The doctor shook my hand and said he was off to get help.

By now, the pirates were growing restless to go out and find the treasure. But there was a question in Silver's mind. He asked himself why the treasure map should have been given to him, and he could think of no good answer. He knew that somewhere there was a trick, and he dared not let the pirates guess his thoughts. We sat round the fire eating breakfast. Silver chatted away, telling the pirates how rich they would all be once they had found the treasure. He painted such a picture that I thought he believed his own words.

We set out with picks and shovels to find
Captain Flint's treasure. The men were
armed to the teeth. Silver had two guns and
a cutlass. As I was a prisoner, I had a rope
tied round my waist and Long John held
the other end. In spite of his promise to keep
me safe, I did not trust him. As we went,
the men talked about the chart. On the back
of it was written:

"Tall tree, Spy-glass Shoulder,
bearing a point to the N. of
N.N.E.
Skeleton Island E.S.E. and by E.
Ten feet."

So we were looking for a tall tree on a
hill. The men were in high spirits and Long
John and I could not keep up with them.
From time to time I had to help him when
his crutch slipped on the stony hillside.

We had gone about half-a-mile when there was a shout from one of the men in front. The others ran towards him, full of hope. But it was not treasure he had found. At the foot of a tree lay a human skeleton.

The silent men looked down in horror. The few rags of clothing that hung on the bones showed that the man had been a sailor. The skeleton was stretched out straight, the feet pointing one way and the arms, raised above the head, in the opposite direction. 'This here's one of Flint's little jokes!' cried Silver. 'These bones point E.S.E. and by E. This is one of the men he killed and he's laid him here to point the way!'

The men felt a chill in their hearts, for they had all lived in fear of Flint. 'But he's dead,' said one of them. 'Ay, sure enough he's dead and gone below. But if ever a ghost walked, it would be Flint's.'

'Ay,' said another. 'I tell you, I don't like to hear "Fifteen Men" sung now, for it was the only song he ever sang.' Silver put an end to their talk and we moved on, but I noticed that now the men spoke softly and kept together. Even the thought of Flint was enough to fill them with terror. At the top of the hill we rested. In whispers, the men still talked of Flint.

'Ah, well,' said Silver, 'you praise your stars he's dead.'

Suddenly from the trees ahead, a thin, trembling voice struck up the well-known song:

'Fifteen men on the Dead Man's Chest –
Yo-ho-ho and a bottle of rum!'

The men were rooted to the spot. They stared in front of them in terror. Even Silver was shaking, but he was the first to pull himself together.

'I'm here to get that treasure!' he roared. 'I was never feared of Flint in his life and, by the Powers, I'll face him dead!'

Long John Silver gave them all fresh heart and they picked up their tools and set off again. We soon saw ahead a huge tree that stood high above the others. The thought of what lay near that tree made the men's fears fade and they moved faster. Silver hobbled on his crutch. I could tell from the evil in his eyes that, if he got his hands on the gold, he would cut our throats and sail away.

The men now broke into a run, but not for long. They had come to the edge of a pit. In the bottom lay bits of wood and the broken handle of a pickaxe. It was clear for all to see that the treasure had gone! The pirates jumped down into the hole and began to dig with their hands. Silver saw his danger. He knew that they would turn on him at any moment.

'We're in a tight spot, Jim,' he whispered.
The look of hate in his eyes had gone. With
the pirates against him, he needed me
again. Once more he had changed sides.
The pirates scrambled out of the pit and
stood facing Silver and me. The leader
raised his arm to charge but before a blow
was struck, three musket shots rang out and
two pirates fell. The three men left ran for
their lives. From out of the wood ran the
doctor and Ben Gunn who had saved us in
the nick of time.

Silver and I were taken to Ben Gunn's cave where the rest of our party were waiting. It was a happy moment for me to see all my friends again. We now learned the answer to the question that had puzzled Silver and me. Dr Livesey had found out that Ben Gunn, alone on the island for so long, had discovered the treasure and taken it to his cave. The map was then useless. My friends were glad to move out of the log-house to the safety of Gunn's cave. That morning, Ben Gunn had watched from the woods as the pirates set out to seek for treasure. It was *his* voice that had struck chill into their hearts with his ghostly song!

That night, the captain, still weak from his wounds, Squire Trelawney, Dr Livesey and the rest of us, feasted and laughed and rested. Long John Silver, quietly smiling, became the polite and willing seaman I had first known.

The next day we started to load the treasure aboard the *Hispaniola* and in a few days were ready to sail. We knew there were three pirates still on the island and we left food and tools for them so that they could last until some ship would one day find them.

And so we set sail. I cannot express the joy I felt to be turning my back on Treasure Island. We had not enough crew to sail the ship home and so we made for the nearest port in South America to get some extra men. We dropped anchor and went ashore, happy to be once again in a bright, busy place. It was nearly dawn when the doctor, the Squire and I returned to the *Hispaniola*. Ben Gunn met us and told us that Silver had left the ship. He had taken a small amount of the treasure and gone. We were all glad to be rid of him. Our one wish now was to reach Bristol safely.

We had a good voyage home. When we arrived, we shared out the treasure and settled back into our daily lives. Ben Gunn got a thousand pounds which he spent or lost in less than three weeks. The Squire gave him a little job in the village and he still sings in the church choir.

Long John Silver has gone right out of my life but sometimes, in a bad dream, I fancy I hear the screeching of his parrot, Captain Flint, 'Pieces of eight! Pieces of eight! Pieces of eight!'

Stories . . . that have stood the test of time

SERIES 740
FABLES
Aladdin and his wonderful lamp
Ali Baba and the forty thieves
Famous Legends (Book 1)
Famous Legends (Book 2)
A first book of Aesop's Fables
A second book of Aesop's Fables
La Fontaine's Fables:
The Fox turned Wolf
Folk Tales from around the World

LADYBIRD CHILDREN'S CLASSICS
Treasure Island
Swiss Family Robinson
Secret Garden
A Journey to the Centre of the Earth
The Three Musketeers
A Tale of Two Cities
Gulliver's Travels
The Lost World

Ladybird titles cover a wide range of subjects and reading ages.
Write for a free illustrated list from the publishers:
LADYBIRD BOOKS LTD Loughborough Leicestershire England